FLORENCE MAYBRICK.

AS SHE APPEARED IN COURT

A THRILLING ROMANCE.

LONDON : G. PURKESS. 286. STRAND. W.C.

FLORENCE MAYBRICK
GUILTY OR NOT GUILTY?

A THRILLING ROMANCE OF REAL LIFE.

PROLOGUE.

IT is the morning of the 7th of August, 1889, and the Court of the Liverpool Assizes is crowded to excess ; whilst outside the court-house hundreds of persons, unable to gain admission, are standing about in groups discussing the bearings of the solemn trial going on within, and speculating curiously on the probabilities of the acquittal or death sentence of the prisoner.

The prisoner in question is a woman—young, comely, and dignified ; and dressed in the sable garb of widowhood.

She is the cynosure of all eyes in that densely-packed court, as she sits in the felon's dock (attended by a harsh-visaged warder) pale and sad, but with an expectant, nay, even hopeful, light in her large, eloquent eyes, and her little gloved hands crossed meekly one over the other.

The mother of two tender and beloved children, she is convicted of intrigue and criminal intercourse with a lover, and accused of the wilful murder of her husband by the administration of poison.

But as the sympathising spectator gazes upon that *petit*, dainty form, the clear-cut, winsome face, and cultured air of grace and refinement, one can scarcely associate such rare tributes with so fearful and hideous a crime.

Surely there must be some mistake—some flaw in the testimony of her accusers ?

The medical evidence in the matter is certainly most conflicting. One party alleges that the prisoner's husband died from natural causes, while the other that his death was due to arsenical poisoning, supposed to have been abstracted from a quantity of fly-papers, and administered to him by his wife.

But, as the learned counsel for her defence justly observed—

"The evidence of the trained nurses (whom the brother of the deceased procured to depose the wife in her attendance upon the sick man, owing to his unkind and unwarrantable suspicion of his sister-in-law) candidly confessed that it was impossible for the prisoner to have administered during their attendance the presumed poison found in the body of the deceased."

And previous to their advent all attempts on the part of the prosecution had signally failed to prove that the hapless prisoner had administered poison to her husband, while it was universally known by his friends and acquaintances that the deceased was an habitual arsenic-taker.

Yet in the face of all these facts the hapless woman was sentenced to death.

The fatal word, "Guilty," was heard with intense astonishment by the spectators, and the murmur that ran through the court indicated a strong feeling of dissatisfaction.

Upon the prisoner the effect was almost electrical.

She had been, of course, removed from the dock while the jury were deliberating ; and on returning, accompanied by a second female warder, she resumed her seat.

When the fatal verdict was pronounced, she half started from her chair, and then, bending forward, buried her face in her hands.

For a brief space the unhappy prisoner's emotion was respected ; then the judge, in a low voice, bade the clerk call upon her.

The clerk rose, and addressing the prisoner, said—

"The jury have convicted you of wilful murder. Have you anything to say why sentence of death should not be passed upon you according to law ?"

Again a buzz of feeling pervaded the court.

The prisoner stood up ; the wonderful nerve she had evinced all through the trial came once more to her aid.

Grasping the rail of the dock, she looked the judge steadily in the face, and with a determined effort, said—

" I wish to say on oath—"

But the noise proceeding from the intense feeling which the startling verdict had evoked prevented the next words being heard.

However, the purport of her words was that, although guilty of adultery, she was innocent of the crime of murder.

A deathlike stillness now fell upon the trembling, sobbing court as the judge, with solemn, awe-inspiring air, assumed the fatal black cap.

Then speaking with awful distinctness, though not unmingled with emotion, he said—

" The law left him no discretion but to pass the sentence which the law directed."

Then followed the prescribed form, closing with the words—

"And may the Lord have mercy on your soul !"

The unhappy prisoner, her head bowed upon her hands, stood clinging to the dock rails.

At a motion of the principal gaoler, the female attendant touched her softly upon the arm.

In a moment the prisoner's dignified air of injured innocence and resentment returned to her.

And scorning the warder's proffered aid, she walked alone, and apparently without tremor, for the last time down the steps to the condemned cell below.

Whether the unhappy prisoner was culpable, or a victim, like many others, of circumstantial evidence, the readers of the following story, founded on this all-engrossing subject, must determine for themselves.

CHAPTER I.

A GLIMPSE OF THE PAST—THE SCHOOLFELLOWS—A SINGULAR CONVERSATION—THE STOLEN LETTER—THE GIPSY'S PROPHECY—THE VICTIM OF TREACHERY.

IT is the summer of 1880. Two young girls, recently arrived from America, are seated at the window of the Royal Hotel, ——mouth, overlooking the restless and ever-changing sea.

They are friends and schoolfellows; both are dark and *distingué* looking.

The eldest of the two, Ida Leverstone by name, is of the Amazon type of beauty—with a superb figure and a magnificent bust, a ravishing complexion, with just a suspicion of " make up " about it, and perfectly classical features, the expression of which, however, was rather calculated to dazzle and intoxicate than inspire the tender passion.

Her companion was her very antipodes; slight, sylph-like, and graceful, with soft, clear-cut features, large, dreamy, expressive blue eyes, and a charm of voice and manner that was simply irresistible.

"How the time passes," observed the classical beauty, stretching her luxurious length on the soft velvet seat, and dropping a fragrant rose she had been toying with. " Fancy, just a week ago to-day since your romantic adventure round the beach yonder. You were near as a toucher food for the fishes, Flo, girl."

"That's so," returned Florence, a little gravely. " I could manage a boat well enough on our smooth American rivers, but I was entirely out of my reckoning on these choppy English seas."

" You'll get used to them in time, Flo, I reckon."

" I guess so ; but, truth to tell, since that little upset I've turned a bit of a coward, and am somewhat afraid to make a second venture. I really thought it was all over with me, Ida."

" And it would have been, Flo, that's certain, but for the ready bravery of the gallant owner of that smart little yacht that was passing at the time."

"Ah! Ida, I shall never forget his noble kindness," murmured Florence, gratefully.

"He's very rich, I've heard since, is this Mr. Jasper Loftus," said the Amazon-like beauty, with strangely flashing eyes. " Owns over a hundred ships and employs nearly a thousand hands."

"Yes," replied Florence in a pre-occupied way.

"And I guess from his style, Flo, the ancient coon is dead spoons on you. Now there's a chance for you, and if you only play your cards right you can hook him as safe as the dollars in the bank."

" Say, Ida, didn't I tell you ?"

" Tell me, what ?"

" That on Mr. Loftus rescuing me from a watery grave," rejoined Florence, seriously, " I remarked that for the noble service he had rendered me I would owe him a debt of gratitude which I feared I should never be able to repay."

"A cheap and easy way of shuffling out of the obligation !" laughed the proud, imperious beauty. " And what said your old man—I mean god of the sea ?"

" That I could repay him by becoming his wife. He would ask for no better reward, and would make me queen of his heart and his vast wealth," said Florence, with a queer little laugh.

" You lucky little puss !" said Ida, enviously. " What a splendid chance ! To be sure he is only a commoner, and a bit rough in his way ; but then he has a noble mind, a generous heart, and, what is better than all, unlimited wealth. Well, Flo, and what was your answer ?"

" I promised to let him know, poor fellow, this very day by post. And that reminds me," she added, suddenly. " Have you any paper and envelopes, Ida ?"

" Heaps," returned Ida ; " do you want them now ?"

" Please, or I shall be too late for the post," said Florence.

Ida rose, and going to a side table, detached a small key from the glittering appendages that hung from her shapely waist, and with it unlocked a dainty inlaid desk.

Taking a package from whence, she tossed it lightly on the table at which her companion was seated, saying—

" Help yourself, my dear."

Then she threw herself into her seat again, and continued to watch the play of the sunlit waves.

Unfastening the packet, Florence held up the contents, exclaiming, with a little silvery laugh—

" Do you expect me to write a love-letter on fly-papers, Ida ?"

" I guess I've given you the wrong packet, Flo," said the resplendent Ida, echoing her friend's laugh.

"I reckon you just have," returned Florence ; 'but what do you want them for—especially such a quantity? I never heard you complain that you were troubled with flies."

" How delightfully innocent and childlike you would like me to think you," said Ida, with an incredulous look under her eyes at her friend ; " do you mean to say you don't know ?"

" No, really, Ida !"

" Is it possible ?" said Ida, still dubious. " Well, I will tell you, Miss Innocence. I soak them and mix the solution with elder water, and it makes a splendid wash for the complexion !"

" Ah ! now I remember the girls at the school in Germany I went to talking about fly-papers for a wash, though I never used it myself."

" But there is another and more potent use to which they can be put, besides that of killing flies and beautifying the complexion," said Ida, significantly, cautiously looking first towards the door, then out of the window, and sinking her voice to a whisper.

" Indeed !" said Florence, a little awed in spite of herself at the sinister and impressive change in her friend's manner.

" Yes," went on the adventuress ; " if your lover should prove troublesome, or your husband old or irksome, a few drops of the solution from those papers in his food occasionally would soon relieve you of the encumbrance, dear."

"Horrible !" exclaimed Florence, recoiling as though at the presence of some beautiful serpent endowed with the power of speech. "Surely no one has ever been guilty of such a fiendish deed ?"

"Haven't they, though," sneered Ida, with a strange, stony look ; "and a great many more will be guilty of it, too, before the world is many years older, I reckon, or I know nothing of human nature."

Shocked and horrified as she was at the terrible revelation, Florence little dreamed how fearfully prophetic her companion's words would prove.

Or rather, how in after years the suspicion of her being guilty of a like crime would fall like a blight upon her, and hopelessly and eternally ruin and embitter her whole life.

Having finished her letter, Florence sealed it, and, putting on her hat, hastened towards the door.

"Shall I come with you, dear ?" said Ida, rising.

"Yes, if you like," returned Florence ; "but you must make haste, for there is only just time to catch the last post."

"In that case, I will meet you on your way back," said Ida, languidly, admiring her exquisite form in the large mirror.

Florence tripped down the carpeted stairs, and was speeding along the picturesque high-street the next instant. A few minutes later a waiter entered the room bearing a letter upon a salver.

"A letter for Miss Chanler," he said, respectfully, and, bowing, left the room.

"Is it from her mother, or an admirer ?" said Ida, picking the dainty, rose-coloured missive up. "The latter, I should think," with a low, sly laugh.

She regarded the superscription closely a minute, then the angry blood flushed into her cheek, and she said, incisively—

"'Tis his. I should know your handwriting, Mr. James Douglass, among a thousand. So this sly, baby-faced, little milksop is trying to supplant me in his affections, is she ? Trying to secure the rich cotton merchant for herself. If it should prove so, let her beware !"

And for an instant her face wore the expression of a beautiful fiend.

One hasty glance around the room to assure herself that she was not observed, and she tore open the envelope, which, crumpling up, she thrust into her pocket.

Eagerly she devoured every word of the fatal letter—fatal to her peace and to that of her so-called friend.

Her brow grew black as night as she read ; her white bosom heaved tumultuously with the vengeful fires that raged within, while her black, evil eyes literally flashed forth fire.

"The cunning, crafty, two-faced viper !" she at length hissed, with concentrated passion. "She thinks to hoodwink and outwit me ; but, by the powers above ! I will circumvent her, or I'll brand myself a fool for evermore."

Concealing the letter in the bosom of her dress and removing all traces of her recent perturbation,

she put on her hat, and, assuming a serene and smiling demeanour, left the hotel.

Meanwhile, Florence, having posted her letter, bent her steps along the beach in the direction of home.

As she was passing the mouth of a deep cleft in the rocks, arched overhead like a cavern, a figure darted out and greeted her with the well-known cry of—

"Cross my hand with silver, fair lady, and I will tell you your fortune !"

Florence would have passed on, but there was something in the voice and manner of the gipsy that seemed to command her attention.

She was of the true Romany type—young, pretty, with splendid teeth, hair, and eyes, and a voice of singular impressiveness and silvery sweetness.

Florence suffered the gipsy to lead her into the recess and take her unresisting hand.

The sibyl looked at it with deep scrutiny for some seconds, and as she further traced the netting of fine delicate lines on the little white palm her dusky brow became alternately elevated or contracted, and at length, placing her beautifully-shaped nail upon a certain line, she said, in a hollow, constrained voice—

"This line points to a violent and terrible death !"

The delicate, sensitive girl shuddered visibly, and instinctively withdrew her hand.

But the gipsy still retained it, and, intently regarding it once more, she added—

"Yet, stay, there is a line—ever so faint—that travels alongside the line of Fate, and—and crosses —yes, at the fatal junction."

"And what does that indicate ?" asked Florence, deeply impressed by the gipsy's manner in spite of herself.

"That the terrible danger which threatens you will be averted even at the eleventh hour," said the sibyl, with awe-inspiring solemnity, "unless the signs read falsely !"

"But the nature of the danger which you say is about to menace me ?" asked Florence, with quavering breath and wildly-beating heart.

"Is a fearful one," replied the gipsy. "You will be accused of a crime, the most hideous, the most insidious and cowardly, and that, too, against one you love and cherish with all the fervour of your being."

"Oh ! this is terrible," panted the deeply agitated girl, trembling in every limb. "You are but jesting with me, surely, or you do not read aright ?"

"The lines seldom lie," said the gipsy, with a half sad, half scornful smile. "But fear not," she added, her beautiful eyes lighting up, "you will come scathless out of this bitter, racking trial, your enemies will be confounded, and your innocence clearly established."

Florence felt for her purse, and seemed anxious to be gone. Reading the action, the gipsy retained her hold and said—

"One moment, lady—the riddle is scarcely read," still closely following the strangely crooked and interesting lines of her fair customer's hand. "Here is a bright period of peace and happiness for you—a fond husband's devotion—the tender clinging love of beauteous children, that will be born to you, and— Ah ! then the dark haunting shadow again crosses your path. The serpent again enters your paradise. It assumes the form of a man—a stranger.

"Avoid him as you would the plague, the breath of the deadliest pestilence, for he will tempt and lure you to the brink of destruction. The cloud again—the blighting, withering omen of fatal strife. This time it takes the form of a woman ; beware of her as you would the most noxious, most venomous reptile, for there is black, ghastly death in her very touch, though 'tis a guised hand that deals the crashing blow. Beware of her, I say, for she is your secret and bitterest enemy, and will be so to the terrible end.

"But I will read no more," concluded the gipsy, huskily, dropping the terrified Florence's trembling hand. "A destiny fraught with such fearful trial and bitter tribulation is seldom crowded into one brief, hapless life.

"Yet despair not," concluded the bright-eyed sibyl, suddenly, and with tender pity in her tones. "The hope held out in the beginning of my reading is still left thee ; cherish it, cling to it as a star of hope, for it may yet save thee."

She gently rejected the money which was held out to her, and Florence, seemingly more dead than alive, staggered from the spot.

She had scarcely recovered her self-possession, when he was joined by Ida Leverstone.

"Well, you have posted your letter ?" she said, with assumed cheerfulness. "And have you accepted your elderly, wealthy, good-humoured lover ?"

"No," returned Florence, with a tinge of self-reproach. " I have declined him."

"Rejected him !" cried Ida, sharp'y, sternly knitting her pencilled brows. "And why, pray ?"

"Because I love another."

"Ah ! 'tis so, then," exclaimed the subtle Ida, with flashing eye and compressed lip ; then with an instant change of tone and a softening of manner— "In love, Flo—with whom ?"

"With the companion of our voyage, Ida," returned the unsuspicious girl—" Mr James Douglass."

Her companion checked the fierce torrent of invectives that rose to her lips, and asked, with forced gaiety—

"And does the gentleman return your devoted affection ?"

"He does, and, moreover, has asked me to become his wife."

"'Tis false, you lying, smooth-tongued little viper !" cried Ida, with flashing eyes, and towering menacingly before her cowering rival.

"This language—and to me !" said Florence, astonished and indignant. "Ida, whatever do you mean ?"

"That James Douglass can never be yours !"

"Indeed ! And why not ?"

"Because I have his written promise offering to make me his wife."

"You ?" exclaimed Florence in startled incredulity.

"Yes, I !" cried Ida, with forcible emphasis. "And who has a better right to the title ?"

"Right !" repeated Florence, with a swelling breast and troubled look. "What claim have you upon him ?"

"The best of all claims," rejoined the triumphant beauty, unblushingly. "He is the father of my unborn child."

This startling revelation came upon the stunned and astounded Florence with the force of an electrical shock.

Confident as she was of the sterling truth and worth of her lover, and utterly false and scurrilous as she believed Ida's statement to be, yet she staggered under the blow as though smitten with a scathing iron. Recovering herself with an effort, however, she gasped out—

"I cannot believe him capable of such base duplicity—such despicable villainy and treachery."

"Nor is he guilty of any of these towards me ; but with you—well, it was certainly not kind—he has been guilty of carrying on a meaningless conversation."

"I'll not believe it !" panted poor Florence. "Your proof !"

"'Tis here !" said Ida, triumphantly, handing her rival the stolen letter.

Florence, with shaking hands, unfolded it, and with trembling lips read as follows—

"MY DARLING PET,—No barrier now exists to prevent me fulfilling my promise of making you my own dear wife. Oh ! how feverishly anxious I look forward to that blissful period when I can call you all my own. In pity to my tortured feelings let not the precious date exceed the end of this month ; though I would have you keep our secret, dearest, till the very last, especially from your supposed friend, Miss ——, whom to my thinking is no fit companion for such as my own dear, darling pet. She is a dangerous woman, I'm afraid—in short, an adventuress, who would not hesitate at magnifying an act of courtesy on my part into a case for the law-courts, in order to secure damages, &c. Trusting to have a note by return, arranging a speedy meeting, I remain, dearest, yours wholly, and for ever,   "J. D."

The unhappy girl staggered against the cliff with a little moan of anguish.

"Now, are you satisfied ?" said her defiant rival, in bitter scorn, snatching the letter from the other's grasp. "He is a man of taste and discernment, and was not to be gulled or bought over by your fawning, meretricious advances and importunities."

"I could never have believed him so base, so false, so utterly depraved," wailed the deeply-stricken girl, in accents of touching grief and despair.

At that instant a firm foot was heard approaching on the shingly beach.

"Come, dry your hypocritical tears," cried Ida, wrathfully. "If you are ambitious to make an exhibition of yourself I've no desire to be thought a party to the show. Someone is coming this way."

Florence drew herself up with the dignity of an insulted queen, and with her handkerchief dashed away her falling tears.

Another minute and Jasper Loftus, the rich ship-owner, stood before her.

He was a fine, tall, good-humoured-looking man of fifty, with golden-brown curly hair and beard, and a bronzed, healthy complexion.

He raised his hat at sight of the ladies, but before he was able to address them Florence, chagrined and distracted by her supposed wrongs, darted impetuously forward, and grasped Mr. Loftus's hand, saying, almost hysterically—

"Oh! Mr. Loftus, I am delighted to see you. Have you come for your answer?"

"Well, Miss Chanler, I—"

He paused awkwardly, and went rosy-red to the roots of his curly hair. He was so taken aback by the abrupt question that for the moment he was unable to frame a reply.

Without heeding his embarrassment Florence went on, rapidly—

"If you are willing to accept my hand in recognition of the service you rendered me, it is yours."

"Become my wife? You amaze me!" blurted out the gallant sailor, gazing in open-eyed astonishment at the little white hand lying in his big brown palm. "Surely, this must be a dream? My wife, say you —when?"

"At once! To-morrow, if you wish it?" returned Florence, distractedly. "What matters it? You saved my life, and who so fully entitled to it as you?"

"Can I credit the evidence of my senses?" said Jasper Loftus, with a half-doubting, dazed, delighted stare. "My wife? Oh! you are an angel sent by Heaven to accomplish my happiness."

And in an ecstacy of uncontrollable joy he was about to enfold her in an impassionate embrace, but she waved him off, saying—

"I must leave you now, for I have a task to accomplish which must not be put off; but to-morrow at noon I will meet you, and be yours for ever 'till death do us part.'"

And like one under the influence of some subtle magnetic power, she turned suddenly and hurried from the spot.

That night she wrote to her lover, bidding him an eternal farewell.

CHAPTER II.

THE WAYSIDE INN — THE INVALID — THE TRAVELLERS—THE STORM—A FATEFUL MEET-ING—A BITTER PARTING.

'TIS the evening of the third day following the events related in the former chapter, and the sky is dark and lowering with every indication of a coming storm.

Florence Chanler and Jasper Loftus are now man and wife. They have been married at a registry office, and are now on their way to the latter's lovely island home at V——.

At a romantic little seaside inn, called the Swan, not many miles distant, James Douglass is staying to recruit his health previous to his departure for the Balearic Islands, whither he is going with a vague idea of doing business (for he is a cotton merchant), and a reckless desire to place as much distance between himself and his native land as possible, for the letter from Florence, bidding him give up all thoughts of her, and wishing him an eternal farewell, has proved a great blow to him, and seriously affected his health.

Seated in the best room the Swan can boast of, the invalid is attended by the worthy host and hostess, Mr. and Mrs. Blandford, who are personally acquainted with the wealthy cotton merchant.

"I hope I shall be able to resume my journey to-morrow," said Douglass, in a languid, despondent way.

"Don't think about it, sir," rejoined the host. "Now that you are better you'll be able to do justice to my larder."

"The vessel on board which I have taken my passage sails in five days. The doctor says I may venture."

"Aye! sir, it was lucky for you to find an old friend in him under the circumstances."

"Yes, indeed, Blandford," said Douglass. "His friendship, his kindness, has effected what his skill would have failed to do."

"He says you're going to catch the plague, sir. I hope you won't come back and give it to us."

"Shall I ever come back? Ah!" said Douglass, mournfully.

"Of course you will, sir."

"This letter," pursued the invalid, producing one as he spoke, "is of the utmost importance. Can it go to-night?"

"Yes, sir. The postman calls here in an hour."

"You will not forget to post it?" said Douglass.

"Give it to me, Mr. Douglass," said Mrs. Blandford, taking the proffered letter. "I will place it here, then I shall be sure not to forget it," sticking it in the frame of the chimney-glass. "There! Any more orders, sir?"

"I thank you, no," said Douglass, wearily.

"If you want anything, sir, ring the bell," said the host, and he and his wife left the room.

"'You must see me no more—we part for ever,' she said, in her cruel, crushing letter," mused the invalid, bitterly. "Vainly have I tried to guess the cause of the change in her feelings towards me, though I feel convinced it is in some way to do with that false, hollow-hearted woman, Ida Leverstone. But I will obey my darling Florence, though it may break my heart; but it will prove that it is hers, and hers alone."

Here Mrs. Blandford entered, saying, as she advanced—

"If you please, sir, some travellers have just arrived, and, as this is our only sitting-room—"

"I understand, Mrs. Blandford," replied Douglass. "I will return to my chamber."

He rose with difficulty.

"I am weak," he added, faintly. "Your arm, madam."

The landlady gave him her arm, and, as she led him towards the door, said—

"The doctor says that writing those letters will be the death of you. It's no use his prescribing if you will write those long letters."

"I am afraid he is right," said the invalid, as he crossed to his room.

He had scarcely gone when the landlord again

appeared, ushering in Jasper Loftus and Florence, who were dressed in travelling costume, the rear brought up by Tom, the waiter, bearing tea equipage, which he placed upon the table near the fire.

"This way, Mr. Loftus," said the landlord, who seemed to be on speaking terms with his visitor. "This way, ma'am," to Florence ; "you'll be more comfortable here than in the public room among the wet visitors."

"Ah ! to be sure," said the happy bridegroom. "I suppose, Blandford, you had no idea of seeing me in your house to-day, and in such company?" affectionately indicating Florence, who had seated herself dreamily by the fire, and to whom he showed the most devoted attention.

"You generally come alone, sir," said the host, "unless your cousin, Mark Hackman, comes with you. A strange man is Mr. Mark, though good at bottom, I should think. Will you occupy the red room as usual ?"

"I can stay but an hour, unless the storm gets worse. I am anxious to reach home."

Then turning to Florence, he added, placing her chair nearer the fire and throwing on more wood—

"There, warm yourself, my dear."

"Ah ! sir, you've got some fine farms at V——, and some capital craft in the harbour," said the landlord.

"Yes," replied Loftus, good humouredly ; "the country is very beautiful, to be sure, and as the whole belongs to me I naturally fancy it cannot be surpassed."

Just then the wind-driven rain beat heavily against the window-panes.

"Is the young lady anxious to proceed ?" said the host. "The weather is getting rough."

"The lady is anxious to enter her husband's house," whispered the delighted Jasper in the host's ear. "Don't you think her husband a lucky fellow, eh ?"

The landlord was about to reply, when at that instant a vivid flame of lightning flashed into the room, followed by a terrific clap of thunder.

"Pardon me," said Florence, in some alarm, "but if I do not crave too much I should wish to stay here the night. The weather frightens me."

"Stay here, my dear?" said Jasper Loftus, eagerly. "Certainly."

"Do not smile at my weakness," continued Florence. "I was always terrified at the sound of thunder."

"Stay here?" said her fond husband, handing her a cup of tea ; "to be sure, my dear. Do just as you please."

"Tom," said the business-like host to the waiter, "go and see that the red room is ready."

"Yes, sir," and Tom departed.

"You need repose, Florence," said Jasper, softly, again leaning tenderly over her chair. "You have been so hurried, so occupied, that you had scarcely time to bid adieu to your friends. You will forgive the haste ?"

She nodded her head wearily and faintly smiled.

"I own I am anxious to show you my home, my craft, my meadows, my Cousin Mark and his wife and boy. He is not like me, a son of the ocean, but a cultivator of the earth—strange, dreamy, but generous. I burn to show him the new treasure I have acquired since I left them—my wife !"

"Your wife, sir ?" gasped the host, who had overheard the last word. "Is that lady—"

"My lawful wife," said Jasper, proudly. "You may stare. Ah ! you would never have thought that one so young and beautiful would have accepted me. I can scarcely believe it myself—it is so like a dream."

Then seating himself beside her, and taking her hand in his, he added, with increased fervour—

"Ah ! Florence, when I beheld you for the first time (when the greedy waves threatened to engulph you), so like a bright vision of the sky, I exclaimed inwardly, 'Happy will be the husband of her choice.' Little did I think—oh ! no, my presumption never extended so far—that I could ever call you mine. I feel proud—proud of myself—and so happy that I am nearly frantic. You will forgive me—I—"

Here the landlady made her appearance.

"Well, wife," said the host, "how is our patient ?"

"Is anyone ill ?" inquired Florence, in order to conceal the embarrassment which her husband's impassioned words had caused her.

"Yes, madam," said the landlady ; "but he is not so bad as he was, poor young gentleman."

"Have you sent for a doctor?" said the kindly-hearted ship-owner.

"Oh ! yes, and I nurse him myself. We expect the doctor presently."

"As soon as our chamber is ready we'll occupy it," said Jasper Loftus ; "perhaps we disturb the poor fellow. Are you warm enough, Florence ?"

"Yes, thanks," she said, absently.

"Now, Master Blandford, I want you to see that my wife's trunks and boxes are carefully sent upstairs. My wife's !" he added, gleefully. "Did you hear that ? My wife's ! Oh ! what a happy fellow I am."

And leading the way out, he was speedily followed by the rest.

"At last I am alone," said Florence, with ineffable sadness, when they were gone, "and for the first time since the celebration of my marriage I can interrogate my heart. Have I acted wisely? He writes me that his heart is still mine.

"Heaven !" she added, starting up, as a terrible thought flashed through her brain. "Can it be that I am the victim of treachery, and that Ida has tricked and deceived me—is indeed the false friend the gipsy warned me of? If so, what a hapless fate is mine ! Oh ! terrible thought. And yet I feel it is so. Poor—poor James ! what will he say when he learns this marriage? Oh ! he will curse me. Oh ! he will—"

But, overcome with emotion, she leant her unhappy head upon the mantel and wept bitter tears.

Looking up at length, she perceived the letter in the glass.

"Ah ! what do I behold?" she exclaimed. "My name on this letter? Yes, it is his handwriting. He must be near. Oh ! where ?"

"That voice! I was not mistaken. Florence!" exclaimed Douglass, entering at that moment, as though in answer to her words.

"'Tis he!" gasped Florence, placing her hand over her violently beating heart.

"Florence, my Florence, how could you have been so cruel?" he cried, advancing and taking her hands.

"How pale, how feeble you are, James!"

"Do not pity me. Florence. I see you—I am happy, my sufferings are gone, my hand touches yours. I am delirious with joy. I can die now happily."

"Die, James? Oh! no, live."

"I will, and for thee, my Florence," and he clasped her passionately to his breast. ...

"James," she panted, faintly struggling to release herself, "forbear—forbear. I beseech you."

"My own dear Florence!" he exclaimed, releasing her instantly.

"Oh! no—not yours," she replied. mournfully. "You must not love me, you must not think of me—it would be a crime. It must not be!"

"A crime to love Florence, who loves me? My senses are wandering—I am still suffering from delirium! I—"

"Someone approaches!" said Florence, hastily. in trembling anxiety. "Should he see you here!"

"He—whom?"

"Depart, I entreat you."

"Why, Florence, what is it makes you tremble so?"

"My—my—"

"What?" he asked. eagerly.

"My husband." she cried, in a stifled voice.

"Your husband!" exclaimed James Douglass, huskily. "Married! Oh! false, cruel, heartless woman!"

And thrusting her violently from him, he hastened to his chamber.

In another moment Jasper Loftus came lightly into the room.

"All is ready, Florence." he said, touching the half-frenzied girl upon the shoulder.

"And we depart at once?" returned Florence, sharply.

"Depart!" he cried, in astonishment. "You forget, Florence, that you expressed a wish to remain here for the night."

"Remain here for the night?" she said shuddering. "Oh! impossible."

"But think of your fatigue, and the storm."

"It has abated." she replied, although at that moment a clap of thunder heavier than all the rest burst over the building. "Oh! sir, let us depart at once," she added, distractedly. "I am no longer alarmed."

"What means this sudden change?" he asked, suspiciously. "The moment I yield to your request you change your mind. Let me entreat that you remain—at least, till the storm has abated. Remember, this is the first time since our marriage that I have spoken without the presence of a witness—this is the first time I have been alone with you. Suffer me to speak of my happiness—"

"Forbear, sir!" she interrupted. "Another

time. I cannot remain here," she added, looking fearfully at the door of James' room. "In mercy, let us depart, I entreat you!"

"A childish whim!" said her husband. "I am not accustomed to the ways of the high world, and, therefore, do not understand the conventionalities of fashionable life. You know the difference of our positions—you shall dictate to me. At twenty my passion would have been violent; but at fifty it has become a perfect worship—idolatry!"

"Oh! should James hear this declaration, he would go mad," she said to herself; then aloud—"In pity, sir, take me hence! I am not well."

At that moment the storm increased with tenfold violence.

The raging wind tore open the window, through which the red lightning seemed to leap in fearful flashes.

Florence started back with a cry of horror: but louder still roared the awful thunder without.

Jasper rushed to the window, and with difficulty closed it up again; while Florence flew to the door of her lover's apartment, which had suddenly opened, and, fastening the same, stood breathless before it.

"Florence, come here," said her husband, strangely and suspiciously.

"Mercy—mercy!" cried the unhappy young wife, and falling on her knees at his feet, she swooned away.

CHAPTER III.

THE HOME OF FLORENCE—GILDED MISERY—THE ESTRANGEMENT—THE SNAKE IN THE GRASS—HOPES AND FEARS—THE FATAL LETTER—A CRUSHING BLOW.

NEARLY two months have elapsed since the day of Florence's marriage—of her secret meeting with James Douglass at the Swan Inn, and her subsequent fainting fit through fear of her husband discovering her lover's presence.

But though Jasper Loftus became almost immediately aware of the crushing fact that his young wife had married him out of a far different motive to love. or even gratitude, yet he failed to define the true cause.

They reached their pretty island home at V— the same night, despite the storm.

But a chilling, withering coldness had sprung up between them from that same hour—an ever-widening estrangement, which resulted in their living in separate residences.

The shadows of evening were slowly falling. and dark, portentous masses were driving up from the western horizon, and the foam-tipped waves ran high and wild.

At the garden-gate of a picturesque white house, nestled among the cliff trees, and overlooking the ship-yard of Jasper Loftus, stood a delicate though comely-looking woman of thirty, gazing anxiously out at the darkening sky and the rising waters.

It was Mrs. Ruth Hackman, the wife of Jasper Loftus' cousin, Mark.

"A pretty sea to venture out in!" she soliloquised. "If Mr. Jasper has no regard for his own

Devil—die!" yelled Jasper, presenting his revolver at the head of the quaking villain.

life, I wis he'd have a little more consideration for my husband's than to entice him to bear him company under such dangerous circumstances."

Her meditations were here put an end to by the arrival of a stranger.

The individual in question was no other than the worthy landlord of the Swan.

"Good-evening, madam," he said, with a nod. "I wish to speak to Mrs. Jasper Loftus, or, as she is called, 'The Lady of the Island.'"

"She is not at home," replied Mrs. Hackman, curtly ; adding to herself—"'The Lady of the Island,' indeed !"

"How unlucky !" said Blandford, with a disappointed air. "I particularly wanted to speak to her."

And he took a letter from his pocket.

"That letter is for her, I suppose ?" said the shrewd Mrs. Hackman. "Why, there is no direction on it !"

"That's of no consequence," returned the talkative host. "I know it belongs to her, because she gave it to me herself to forward to a young gent— that is, I mean——"

"A young gentleman !" said Mrs. Hackman, sharply catching him up.

"Who went away to—I don't know where."

"What young gentleman ?"

"Never you mind," said Mr. Blandford, cautiously. "The lady never called again ; and so I thought, as I had business to do in this place, I would bring it back to her own hands, for she told me not to tell. Curse my foolish, slippery tongue !" he mentally rejoined.

"Give me the letter !" said Mrs. Hackman, with suspicious eagerness.

"No, thank you. I've had it a couple of months, and I'll not part with it except to herself."

"But why this mystery ?" said the lady, chagrined at her failure to obtain the missive. "Will you call again, and you shall have something to drink ?"

"Yes, I'll call again. I've put my nag up at the Golden Anchor, and I will return in an hour."

"Very good."

And turning on his heel, Blandford disappeared down the cliff path.

"There is some dark mystery in all this," said Mrs. Hackman, musingly ; "and could I but obtain that letter I should get at the secret."

A footfall was heard behind her, and a moment more her husband stood by her side.

Mark Hackman was handsome, and of gentlemanly appearance, though there was something cruel and treacherous in the shifty expression of his cautious, sleepy-looking eyes. His voice was soft and persuasive, and his manner gentle and cat-like.

"Well, Mark ?" said Mrs. Hackman.

"All's well, Ruth," returned her husband. "Jasper went to the rescue of the Skylark with his usual bravery and generosity, and brought them all safely to shore."

"I am glad of that ; but I was fearful on your account, and on his."

"On his !" said Mark Hackman, significantly. "I can tell you, Ruth, that my affection is very much diminished since that cursed——"

"Marriage of his," put in his wife.

"Exactly. It is not that I mind the money so much, Ruth," said Mark Hackman, with seeming candour (this was utterly false, for money was his sole and only thought—in short, his god) ; "but I am his next-of-kin, and then he is god-father to our son, and promised to make him his heir-at-law."

"To be sure he did, Mark."

"Then, who would have thought," pursued Hackman, "that after the half-savage life he has led for forty years he would go and find a wife, purposely to go and leave all his wealth to her."

And an expression the most sinister passed for a moment over his usually mild, serene features, and he threw himself angrily into a rustic seat.

"And to choose, too, a young lady of fashion— who gives herself airs and graces !" went on Mrs. Hackman. "What does he want with such a wife ?"

"Ay ! indeed—the deceitful fool, the idiot, the cheat !" cried Mark Hackman, with bitter vehemence.

"Do you recollect how she stared when she first entered the house ?" pursued Mrs. Hackman, wrathfully. "You would have supposed she was entering a stable. And when she speaks, how grand she is ! And then the people about here do not content themselves with calling her plain Mrs. Jasper Loftus, like they call me, Mrs. Hackman, but she is called the Lady of V—— forsooth, because she has got a doll's face, and is haughty and proud."

Mark Hackman seemed to pay no attention to this vehement tirade, but remained wrapped in deep thought.

"This is all very pretty for a fine stuck-up miss, who did not bring her husband a penny," pursued Mrs. Hackman ; then, suddenly noticing her husband's abstraction—"What are you thinking of, Mark ?"

"Of the day on which the unhappy bride took from the drawer—by mistake, of course—the paper of deadly poison which we use in the foundry. Why did you not put it out of her way, you stupid fool ?" cried Mark Hackman, fiercely, and with fearful meaning.

"Mark, do you know what you are talking about ?" asked Mrs. Hackman, a terrible suspicion entering her mind.

"Bah ! you have no blood in your veins," retorted her husband, contemptuously. "For my part, I am as frank in my hate as I am in my love ; and I hate this woman."

These last words were uttered with such demoniac intensity and malignity that they both awed and shocked the terrified woman who heard them.

"What !" she exclaimed, in trembling surprise, "hate the wife of your kinsman—your best friend ?"

"He is no friend of mine," hissed Mark Hackman, vengefully. "He's nothing to me or mine. Why did he marry, eh ?"

Mrs. Hackman shook her head ruefully.

"Why did I take care of his money, and lay it out to the best advantage while he was at sea ?" pursued the highly incensed plotter. "His capital is nearly doubled, and yesterday he was mean and contemptible enough to ask for the account-books to make a schedule of his property."

"The suspicious bear !" said Mrs. Hackman, resentfully.

"I have kept no account-books," resumed her husband, "because, thinking his wealth would descend to us, it was unnecessary."

"I must own," said Ruth, "that Jasper Loftus

was more kind to us formerly than he is now, and he has not executed the will in favour of our son, as he said he would."

"Of course not," said Mark Hackman, in a burst of jealous fury. "That accursed marriage has spoilt all. And what has he married ?"

"A woman without the slightest affection for him," said Ruth.

"Ay ! indeed—a mercenary, a cursed interloper, who has come to rob us of our rights ! I have dwelt on it till it has almost driven me mad."

"Moreover," continued Mrs. Hackman, "I strongly suspect her of loving another."

"Loving another !" echoed her husband, with feverish anxiety. "Give me the proof, Ruth—give me the proof !"

"A man has been here," returned Ruth, "Blandford, the innkeeper of the Swan at ——mouth, with a letter from a young gentleman, and he stops at the Golden Anchor."

"A love-letter, perchance," cried Mark Hackman, triumphantly, seizing sharply upon the idea. "If so, the prospects of our son are not quite ruined. I'll turn the letter to profit, or may I be hanged !"

He must have been inspired with prophetic power to have made use of such an expression.

"Hush ! Mark," said Ruth, touching his arm. "She comes this way."

As she spoke, Florence, elegantly attired, appeared descending the steps of her little villa facing them.

"Look at her dress. What extravagance ! She only does it because—"

"I'll spoil her finery," interrupted her husband, menacingly.

Then, as Florence advanced, followed by her manservant, Robert, Hackman said aloud, with his crafty smile—

"Good-day, Cousin Florence ! I hope you are not offended with my freedom ; but we are cousins, you know."

"I know it, sir," said the unhappy girl, courteously but coolly.

"I say, Mark, what grand airs," whispered Ruth in her husband's ear.

"I had requested you, Robert," said Florence, turning to the groom, "to saddle my horse."

"Yes, madam," said the man, bowing, "but the order was countermanded."

"And by whom ?" asked his mistress, her fair brow contracting slightly.

"By me !" said Mrs. Hackman, defiantly.

"And wherefore ?" demanded Florence.

"Because your husband expects company, and it is your duty to stay at home and do the honours of the house," returned Ruth.

"Indeed !" said Florence, her pale cheek flushing with wounded pride. "It seems, madam, in thus addressing me, you presume upon my prerogative." Then, to the servant—"Robert, say to Lucy, my maid, that I do not ride to-day, and bid her prepare my dinner dress."

"I have sent her out on an errand for her master," said Mrs. Hackman, maliciously.

"Really," said Florence deeply offended, "your notions are very strange. You forget that I am mistress of the house."

"Her house ?" muttered Mark Hackman, with a sneer.

"I thought you could do without your maid for once," went on Mrs. Hackford, with undisguised spleen in her tones. "It is not by embroidering flowers or painting butterflies that a house is managed. I am the cousin of Jasper Loftus, and not his servant."

"In your own house you may do as you please—in mine, I command," retorted Florence, with imperious dignity.

"She'll turn us out next," said Mark Hackman, with sarcasm.

"You give yourself mighty airs, madam," said Ruth, blusteringly. "A pretty fuss, indeed, about a lady's maid. Suppose you had not married Jasper Loftus, you must have done without, and you can do so now."

"This is unendurable," said Florence, greatly upset. "Robert, say to your master I wish to speak with him."

"Yes, madam," said the groom, bowing, and departing.

"Where is the man with the letter ?" quietly said Hackman to his wife as they stood apart.

"At the Golden Anchor," she replied, under her breath.

"Good. You've begun the fight for mastery ; I will finish it."

And with these ominous words he hurriedly left the spot.

His wife, rudely turning her back upon the helpless girl, entered her house.

"So much insolence is not to be borne," said Florence, tears of bitter indignation starting to her sad eyes when she was alone. "I must acquaint my husband. But have I the right to claim, to require aught of him ? Will he not answer me that they are the only beings who understand his peculiar temper and habits, the only beings who love him ?

"And can I reply to him," she added, with self-reproach, "that no one understands or loves him better than his wife ? No ; the blush on my cheek would proclaim its falsity.

"Oh ! James, why is your image ever before me ? My letter must have reached him—he knows all, save the name of my husband, alas !"

Robert, the groom, returning, approached his mistress, and said—

"If you please, madam, I cannot find my master but Mr. and Mrs. Raylands have arrived and wish to see you. Here they are," he added, as the visitors appeared.

Mr. Raylands was a dapper little man, with something unmistakably legal about his cut and demeanour, while his wife was a fine, elegantly-formed woman several years his junior.

Florence greeted them warmly.

"Laura, my dear friend !" she said, pressing the lady's hand. "Mr. Raylands, I am happy to see you at V——. How is my mother ?"

"Quite well. I sent you word I was coming, Florence."

"And I wrote a post scriptum to your husband, my dear madam, to that effect," said Mr. Raylands.

"He did not name it to me," said Florence, thoughtfully. "How strange."

Mr. Raylands, having handed their wraps to Robert, that worthy withdrew.

"It was to surprise you, my dear," resumed Mrs. Raylands. "We wrote Mr. Loftus that on our way to the baths we should call upon you."

"But you are altered, Florence," added her friend, regarding her with tender concern. "You look pale and sad. Are you happy? Answer me."

Choking down her emotion with an effort, Florence replied—

"The truth is, my dear Laura, a relative of Mr. Loftus assumes more than she ought in my house, and greatly vexes me. She once managed the establishment, and is unwilling to abdicate her authority."

"Send her away, Florence dear, and her husband with her."

"Mr. Loftus would not permit it," said Florence, with a bitter smile.

"Not permit it, indeed !" returned the lawyer's dainty spouse, assertively. "Does he permit his wife to be insulted ? I should talk to him."

"I tremble before him, Laura."

"My dear, you are very absurd. I never tremble before Mr. Raylands—do I, love ?"

"No, my dear," assented that diminutive limb of the law ; and he muttered to himself, "Rather the other way about."

"I know I am wrong," said Florence. "Mr. Loftus is violent, hasty in temper ; but he is much beloved by his people—his neighbours."

"By his neighbours, forsooth !" reiterated Mrs. Raylands. "Why, is he not beloved in his own house ? Is he disobedient, dear ? Where is your house ?" looking about.

"Lucy and I inhabit that building," said Florence, pointing to the villa.

"Yourself and Lucy !" said the lawyer's wife. "If it's a fair question, dear, does not your husband dwell in the same habitation ?"

"No ; there is his dwelling," said Florence, in a shamefaced way, indicating a small pavilion overlooking the shipyard.

"Already ?" said the lawyer. "This must lead to a divorce."

"Pardon me, my dear," said Mrs. Raylands, "I cannot forbear laughing—I cannot comprehend it. When did this separation commence ?"

"From the day of our marriage," said Florence, with a sigh.

"Why, my dear, you have never been married at all," said her friend, laughing. "But such a state of things cannot last."

"What can I do ?" said Florence, with emotion. "Alas ! I am wretched."

"I will speak to your husband on the matter."

"Pray be careful," said Florence, tearfully. "Mr. Loftus is very eccentric."

"I am quite satisfied of that, my dear Florence," said her friend.

"And remember he is my best client," said the lawyer, warningly.

"Leave the matter in my hands. I'll soon put everything to rights."

"She is quite capable of it," said her husband, confidently. "But see, hither comes Mr. Jasper. Let us retire, my dear madam."

And taking Florence's arm, they re-entered the house.

Jasper Loftus now came upon the scene.

He was followed nearly to the gate by a crowd of sailors, workmen, and their wives and children, who greeted him with loud shouts of—

"Bravely done, Mr. Loftus ! Long life to you, sir ! Hurrah—hurrah !"

He was dressed in easy, negligent, sailor-like fashion, and carrying a boat-hook.

"A strange-looking creature to marry a lady like Florence," thought Mrs Raylands.

"Good-morning, Mr. Loftus," she said, greeting him.

"My dear madam," he replied, raising his hat, "excuse me receiving you in this plight, but I have only just come out of the sea. Twelve poor creatures were in the water. Where is your husband? I have anxiously expected you."

"With Florence," said Mrs. Raylands.

"Why did you leave her ? Let me conduct you to her."

"Presently, sir. I have something particular to speak to you upon."

"With me, madam ?" said the ship-owner, in surprise.

"Yes, with you, sir," said the lady, severely. "Do you think the manner in which you treat your wife calculated to render her happy ? Remember, sir, Florence is my friend—almost my sister."

"Madam !"

"You will not frighten me, Mr. Loftus," said Mrs. Raylands, facing him boldly. "You may frown, but I have been a wife three years, and it takes a good deal to alarm me."

"Go on, madam," said the ship-owner, with assumed calmness.

"And you promise to be calm, though I should ask you why your wife is unhappy ?" said the lawyer's wife.

"Unhappy !" repeated Jasper Loftus, with emotion ; "she unhappy ?"

"Tell me, has Florence forgotten your generosity or failed in her duty ?"

"My generosity—her duty ! Alas !" said he, sighing deeply.

"She received me with a tearful eye and a pallid cheek," went on Mrs. Raylands. "I at once perceived she was not happy. Almost an exile in this corner of the earth, I learn that she is not mistress in her own house, but contemned by those who surround her."

"Madam, I—"

"Don't interrupt me, please. In the name of her friend I ask for an explanation. If you did not love her why did you marry her ?"

"Not love her ?" said Jasper Loftus, with intense feeling. "Heaven is my witness—"

And, overcome with emotion, he sank upon the seat and buried his face in his hands.

"He weeps," said Mrs. Raylands, compassionately. "You are not well, sir. Shall I call for assistance ?"

"No, I beseech you," he said, rising. "I am not ashamed of weeping before you. I can no longer conceal the secret that consumes me."

He paused.

"Proceed, sir."

"You met your friend with a tearful eye and pallid cheek," continued the sorrowing man. "Look at me. Am I what I was ? The blood has forsaken my cheek, and my eye has lost its fire. You said rightly, madam, that happiness was a stranger at my fireside. Every day brings a fresh sorrow, every hour a new torture."

"What can be the reason ?" said Mrs. Raylands, in a puzzled way.

"Because I love my wife, and my wife does not love me," exclaimed Jasper Loftus, with convulsive vehemence.

"Impossible ! You do not understand each other."

"On my bended knees I thanked her for granting me her hand ; she generously cancelled an obligation and accomplished a duty."

This was said with touching pathos, and, after the pause of a moment, he again continued—

"She followed me, madam, but followed as a slave follows its master—as the prisoner follows the gaoler. If I speak of the future—of happiness—of love—she answers me with tears and sobbings. If I attempt to console her she flees from me. She hates me, madam—I am convinced of it."

And he paced the turf in deep perturbation.

"All this is very mysterious," returned Mrs. Raylands, truly perplexed.

"She is the victim of self-sacrifice in some way, I am certain," pursued the millionaire. "I have ceased to complain. When my daily toil is done I retire to my lonely chamber, leaving her undisturbed by my presence. And now, madam, can you comprehend the grief that is consuming me?"

"I have wronged you, sir," said Mrs. Raylands. "Forgive me ! Florence cannot hate you. She does not understand you. All must be explained—all will be well. She will appreciate you as you deserve to be. She, in short, will love you."

"Oh ! say you so ?" exclaimed Jasper, wistfully, brightening up at the gleam of hope.

"I am sure of it," said the genial woman. "A while ago I could have torn your hair out, Mr. Loftus ; now, there's my hand !"

It was a nice, plump white hand, and Jasper pressed it warmly and gratefully.

"I will seek Florence," Mrs. Raylands added, "and heal your differences. Farewell !"

Jasper bowed.

"I declare he is as tractable as a lamb," said the lawyer's wife, as she returned into the house.

"At length my fate is to be decided," said Jasper Loftus, when she had gone. "Florence will be made acquainted with my true feelings. Bright star of hope, in thee I put my trust !"

At this juncture Mark Hackman strode up.

He had been to the Golden Anchor, and under the influence of his insidious tongue and sundry glasses had induced the easy-going host of the Swan to part with the mysterious letter.

"'Tis a love-letter, sure enough," putting his hand in his pocket as he advanced to assure himself it was there.

"Ah ! Mark," said Jasper, catching sight of him. "Do you want me ?"

"Not unless you please," returned Hackman, resentfully. "I can go. I can render up my accounts, and the sooner the better, perhaps."

"And wherefore, pray ?" said his relative in astonishment.

"Because I am going away, that's all."

"You are going to leave me—your friend—your relative ?"

"It is because I am your friend that I ought not to be treated like a servant, nor my wife either," said Mark, broodingly. "She is not a fine lady, to be sure, but she has her valuable qualities. I shall retire on my hard savings."

"You are out of your mind, Mark. I will speak to my wife—all will be well."

"It's of no use," returned the other, doggedly. "I would not stay if she were to ask me."

"If a few hasty words uttered by a young and inexperienced woman," said Jasper Loftus, sternly, "can dissolve an old friendship like ours, I will not detain you."

"Words ! Words would be deemed nothing. But there are deeds from which every honest mind must revolt," said the insidious Mark, with Iago-like subtlety.

"You have a motive, it appears," said Jasper, mistrustfully, "and you wish to conceal it."

"Perhaps I have—perhaps not," said Mark, evasively.

"Between you and I, Mark, there should be no secrets. Speak out."

"Well, then— But there—I don't like," added the base schemer with well assumed reluctance. "No, I will not."

"Tell me at once," demanded Jasper, passionately. "I will know !"

"Well, you love your wife, Jasper, but your wife does not love you," said his cousin with a venomous hiss.

"Who dares to assert it ?"

"Yourself ! Poor fool !" cried Mark, with biting contempt. "You love her with all the passion which she feels for another."

"Liar ! wretch ! coward !" exclaimed Jasper Loftus, in a paroxysm of jealous fury ; and seizing Mark by the throat, shook him violently. "Unsay those false, dastardly words or I will tear your vile tongue out by the roots."

"They are true !" gasped the struggling, panting wretch.

"Devil ! Die !" yelled Jasper, furiously, and snatching a revolver from his hip pocket, he presented it at the head of the quaking villain.

But a startled scream from Florence, who now appeared at the door of the villa, arrested Jasper's deadly intention.

"Your proof, vile defamer—your proof ?" demanded the highly-incensed Jasper, lowering his weapon, "or I will have your wretched life."

"Kill me if you will," cried Mark, in an injured tone. "There, read that! I am neither liar nor villain!" And he presented a letter as he spoke.

Jasper snatched it from his hand.

"A letter—unaddressed—but the name? Ha! yes, I see it all," he added, with terrible consternation and agony in his look. "He must have been near us at the Swan Inn. Blind, infatuated fool that I was! She—she is false, heartless, and I a wretched, disgraced, dishonoured man."

And the great strong man threw himself into a seat and wept like a very child.

Mark Hackman, as if satisfied with the cruel blow he had struck, bestowed upon his suffering victim a glance of fiend-like exultation, then stole with cat-like motion from the spot.

CHAPTER IV.

FLORENCE ATTEMPTS A RECONCILIATION—A STORMY SCENE — A SUBTLE PLAN — THE POISONER BEGINS HIS DEADLY WORK.

EARLY next morning Florence ventured forth to inhale the fresh sea air and collect her deeply-perturbed thoughts.

She had not taken many steps ere she encountered her husband, seated, dejected, upon the old rustic seat.

He was in the same attitude as on the previous evening, and the thought that perhaps he had been there all night struck to her heart in a pang of pity and remorse. She approached, and gently touched him on the arm.

"Ah! sir," she said, tenderly, "you are pale and chilly. I fear you are not well."

"Hypocrite!" muttered her husband, starting as though a serpent had stung him. "But I will know my wronger's name!"

"Why do I tremble before him?" thought the deeply-agitated young wife; then, addressing him, she said, in pleading accents—"Ah! sir, forgive me?"

"Forgive you!" he returned, hoarsely, turning a wan, haggard, accusing face to her.

"I know you have cause to complain of me," she went on; "but you are generous. The future is before us, and my entire devotion must atone for the past; and let me hope the day is nigh—"

"Peace, false perjured woman!" cried Jasper Loftus, fiercely. "Tell me the name of him to whom you addressed this letter?" showing the one he had received from his cousin.

"Ah!" cried Florence, starting, "how came you by it?"

"Dare you interrogate me? Answer my question —his name?"

"I am innocent! Listen to me?" supplicated the unhappy Florence.

"His name, I say—I insist upon knowing it?" thundered Jasper.

"That you may challenge him," retorted Florence, warmly. "Never, sir! You shall not rashly expose your life."

"Hypocrite! it is not for me you tremble—it is for him; and you are right. If I find him I will kill him!" he cried, with terrible earnestness.

"Mercy—mercy!" cried Florence, in terrified accents.

"The Swan Inn!" rushed on her husband. "You concealed him then, and would protect him now. Ah! you see, I know your vile secret. Tell me his name, and I will spare you—his name!"

"I cannot—I cannot, for your sake!" she exclaimed, distractedly.

"Wretched woman!" he cried, pushing her furiously from him. "But, see—your friends approach. Conceal your false tears—as I conceal my bitter, burning shame—as best you may. Heaven help me!"

"My dear Mr. Jasper, we wait for you," said the lawyer, as he came up.

"Pardon me, sir, but—" began Jasper Loftus, in an embarrassed manner.

"Have I not guessed rightly, eh, Mr. Jasper?" said Mrs. Raylands, slyly bestowing upon him an arch look.

"We can understand each other," said Jasper Loftus, with intention. "You must excuse my sitting down to breakfast with you, but matters of importance demand my presence elsewhere."

"Husband, you will not go," said Florence, wistfully—"you will not leave us?"

"You, Florence, will do the honours of the table. I will join you as soon as possible."

The party returned to the house, Jasper Loftus alone remaining behind.

"She conceals his name from me," he mused, "but I can yet satisfy my revenge. At the Swan Inn I can learn all. To the world's end I will follow this detested rival—this destroyer of my peace!"

"Yes," said Mark Hackman, slyly stealing up to him, "you will dare him to follow you to Paris, and you will fight him. He will kill you, marry your widow, and enjoy your property."

"I will prevent the possibility of that, Mark, by making your son Albert my sole heir. A few strokes of my pen will secure all to you and yours, my friend, who could not brook to see me dishonoured."

An eager, greedy light leaped into Mark's evil eyes, and he fervently pressed his relative's hand.

"Oh! Mark, how I hate that woman," added Jasper, with a tearful emotion.

"And yet you weep for her," said the other, wrathfully.

"Yes, like a child," returned Jasper, dashing aside his tears. "Ah! no man ever loved as I love her."

And with a slow and languid step he betook himself to his solitary chamber in the pavilion, near the foundry.

"My son will be his heir," muttered Mark, watching his departing footsteps; "and I shall have no accounts to give up. He will not fight a duel and be killed. No; he will return, see her, and be more infatuated than ever. Then he will call for his accounts, and I shall be lost."

He paused, and remained for several moments in deep thought, then suddenly, and with startling vehemence, exclaimed—

"No, no! Perish the haunting thought! His fortune must be mine—every penny of it! It has been the one dream of my life. I have gone too far to retract now, and, though I had to wade knee-deep in crime, nothing shall turn me from my purpose. The fatal blow must be struck—aye, and speedily, too ; but, though through my agency, it must be dealt by another hand than mine, and the odium rebound on the head of the innocent !"

CHAPTER V.

STRICKEN—THE HAND OF DEATH—THE SECRET ASSASSINS — THE CONSULTATION — HUSBAND AND WIFE—A TERRIBLE ACCUSATION.

THE sickness which had so suddenly seized Jasper Loftus visibly increased, and each day he seemed to get weaker and thinner, and at last, under the joint efforts of his wife and Mrs. Raylands, he was induced to occupy a room in the same house with Florence.

Mr. Raylands, owing to pressure of business, was compelled to return to London ; but his humane, kindly-hearted wife determined to remain with her friend Florence during the strange and mysterious illness of Mr. Loftus.

It was towards daybreak, and the wax tapers, burnt nearly down to their sockets, in the sombre sitting-room scarcely served to dispel the pall-like gloom that struggled with the coming light.

Signs of long and watchful vigils were everywhere apparent about the place, and at a side table, with tea service and writing materials before her, sat the indefatigable Mrs. Raylands.

She was reperusing a letter she had just written, and it ran thus—

"You may congratulate yourself, my dear husband, that you were recalled to London. I cannot quit Florence. Ever since your departure Mr. Jasper has become worse and worse. Thanks to the skill of the doctor and the attention of his wife, the poor patient is a little better, but he seems insensible of her attentions. I shall write again by to-morrow's post.—Yours, &c."

She folded up the letter just as Mrs. Hackman came into the room.

"Up already, madam?" said the latter.

"Inquietude kept me from sleeping," said Mrs. Raylands. "How is the patient?"

"A little better. He would get up, and Mrs. Loftus called me to her assistance. She will kill herself if she exerts herself much more."

"Poor Florence !" said her friend, with a sigh. "She has indeed given proof of her devotion."

"I'll tell you what it is, madam," said Ruth. "Mrs. Loftus is no favourite of mine, but truth is truth. Since her husband's illness she has not left him day or night, and I won't believe a word that is said about her."

"What is said of her?"

"All sorts of things—as wicked and abominable as they are impossible," returned Ruth ; then, impressively—"Remember, madam, she is not the first woman that loved one man and was driven to marry another."

"What do they say?" again inquired Mrs. Raylands.

"You know what I mean, madam. But it is the letter that has caused all the mischief."

"A letter?"

"Yes ; but that does not prove that she wishes her husband dead," said the garrulous Ruth ; and then, sinking her voice to a mysterious whisper, "though everybody says she has poisoned him."

"Horrible !" cried Mrs. Raylands, with a shudder. "But you do not believe it any more than myself? If Mr. Loftus recovers he will certainly have to thank his wife."

"That's what I say to them," replied Ruth Hackman. "But they say it is all assumed to ward off suspicion. Should anything fatal happen to Jasper I dread the consequences."

"How so ?"

"The workmen are exasperated, and would not hesitate to deliver her up to justice."

"Preposterous ! But, hush ! here she comes," said Mrs. Raylands, as Florence, turning the handle, softly stepped into the room.

There were great dark circles under her eyes, and she was wan, and walked with evident fatigue.

"Mrs. Hackman," she said, addressing that lady, "my husband desires me to retire. Robert and Lucy will sit with him, but I rely upon you to call me should it be necessary."

"I will," said Ruth. "But let me watch to-night. You are ill already."

"You are a mother," said Florence, feelingly. "Your child requires your care. I could not permit it."

"That is not the language of a wicked, guilty woman," said Ruth to herself, as she left the room.

"Well, Florence," said Mrs. Raylands, in her genial, pleasant way, "you look terribly pale, and your eyes are quite red for want of sleep."

"My dear Laura, however highly I may prize your friendship I must confess that I wish you were in London. Your husband will be displeased at your stay."

"I cannot leave you, Florence," rejoined Mrs. Raylands, readily, "until your husband's health is restored. The doctor says he has hopes."

"The disease baffles his skill," said Florence, with a troubled look, "and the symptoms perplex him. He will not pronounce him out of danger."

"Should he perish !"

"Perish !" repeated Florence, paling to the very lips and staggering back. "Heaven forbid ! Should he die I should deem myself his murderer."

"His murderer !" exclaimed her friend, regarding her with a perplexed look.

"Yes, my friend—my sister. I will reveal to you a secret. I have deceived my husband."

"Florence, you terrify me," said Mrs. Raylands, starting back.

"'Tis true," said Florence, sadly. "I gave my hand to him, but my heart was entirely another's."

"Gracious Heavens !"

"Devoted to James Douglass, whom I ought not to have seen," said the unhappy girl, with a sob. "Accident threw him in my way at the Swan Inn, ——mouth. I wrote to acquaint him of my marriage. My husband discovered the secret, and the following day saw him on a bed of sickness. Should he die, remorse will kill me."

"Forbear, Florence," said Mrs. Raylands, somewhat alarmed. "Banish your lover from your thoughts ; submit to your husband—you have vowed it at the altar. He will pity and forgive you. Happiness is still within your reach."

The young wife, sighing deeply, said—

"Let us take a short walk upon the beach, the sea air will revive me."

They put on their hats and wraps, and left the house.

Ten minutes later Mark Hackman and his wife Ruth were seated in the room which the ladies had but recently vacated.

"I think, Mark, you need not have gone to the town to hear such shocking rumours," Ruth was saying.

"I tell you for three miles round nothing else is talked of," said her husband. "And had it not been for my interference, the magistrates would have been applied to before this. It is too early yet," he muttered to himself.

"Ah !" sighed Ruth, "if you had seen her devotion, you would never say she was a guilty woman."

"Oh ! never mind her," said Mark, gruffly. " I say, Ruth, has that Doctor Grey been here ?"

"Yes, for the last three days."

"Does he suspect anything, think you ?" asked her husband, strangely.

"I don't know," returned Ruth, pointedly ; "but I have my suspicions."

"You ? What are they ?"

"The packet of poison used in the factory I took from her a month ago and placed in my secret drawer is no longer there."

"Come, now, Ruth," said her husband, persuasively, "Jasper's wife was in the habit of going into your room, wasn't she ?"

"Never !" said Ruth, emphatically.

"But I say she was," declaimed Mark, sternly. "How else could the poison disappear ?"

"Mark," said his wife, regarding him with mingled fear and amazement, "your words are enough to bring her to the scaffold."

"I must say what I think," said the ruffian, darkly. "The packet must be found."

"Of course it must."

There was a silence of some few seconds, which, however, Mark was the first to break.

"You were saying, Ruth, that Jasper got out of bed to-day. He was very bad when I went away."

"He has been inquiring for you. Had you not better see him ?"

"Yes—yes," said her husband, uneasily. "I had better see him now that his wife is not there."

"I'll go and tell him that you have arrived," said Ruth, rising.

"Stay—stay," said Mark, with strange eagerness. "Is he much altered for the worse ?"

"You'd scarcely know him," replied his wife. " I think I hear him stirring. He cannot rest in his bed, and comes here for a little change of scene."

She advanced towards the centre door and threw it open.

There, clinging to the door-post, stood Jasper Loftus.

Hardened villain as he was, Mark Hackman started back in horror at the terrible spectacle which his unhappy relative presented.

His eyes had sunk deep into his head, his cheeks were hollow, and his skin was a ghastly greenish hue, upon which the death-sweats seem gathered, while his once stalwart form was wasted to a mere skeleton, and his clothes hung upon him in folds.

Truly he was a terrible wreck of his former self.

With Ruth's help, and an extreme effort on his own part, he at length reached an arm-chair and seated himself.

"Well, Mark," said he, in a weak, feeble voice when he had recovered his breath, "have you executed my wishes ?"

"I have. Leave us, Ruth."

Mrs. Hackman immediately withdrew.

"Come, Mark, your hand," said the invalid, languidly holding out his wasted fingers. "Am I so altered that you do not recognise me ?"

Mark took his hand reluctantly, but seemed to recoil at the touch. It was so like the hand of the dead, thought the trembling wretch.

"Come nearer, Mark," said Jasper, in a low voice. "Do my looks terrify you ? Help me to reach that glass. Yours is the hand of friendship, Mark."

His treacherous relative assisted him across to the mirror facing them.

Seating himself before it, the hapless sufferer surveyed his changed and fearfully emaciated features a space.

"Ah !" he said, with a mournful shake of the head, "they say I shall recover. Death is imprinted in my face. Well, I have no wish to live. My sufferings are so constant and so acute that it would be a merciful act to kill me."

"Mark," he added, turning away and placing his hand to his parched throat, "a terrible and unquenchable fire burns within me and slowly consumes me !"

"My courage will fail," muttered the conscience-stricken Mark to himself.

"I am thankful that my life has been spared till your return," said the invalid. "To you alone I said Florence was guilty—to you alone I now declare that she is innocent !"

"Innocent ! You have forgotten the letter !" said the vicious, taunting villain.

"On the contrary," returned Jasper, "I have perused it again and again, and am convinced that Florence is a pure and virtuous wife."

Mark bit his lip. The sick man proceeded—

"On the first perusal, jealousy blinded both my judgment and reason ; on calmly reading it I comprehended its import. She loved, and was beloved again."

He paused from weakness a moment, then resumed—

"The letter in question was intended to inform her lover that it would be criminal in him to think more of her, for that she was a wife. She is an angel of purity and goodness, Mark," said Jasper, in conclusion, "and you must bury the past, and treat her with the respect which is her due."